This book belongs to

....

Illustrated by: Dubravka Kolanovic
Reading consultant: Geraldine Taylor

Marks and Spencer plc
PO Box 3339
Chester CH99 9QS

shop online
www.marksandspencer.com

ISBN 978-1-78061-704-6
Printed in China

Cinderella

Five steps for enjoyable reading

Traditional stories and fairy tales are a great way to begin reading practice. The stories and characters are familiar and lively. Follow the steps below to help your child become a confident and independent reader:

Step 1
Read the story aloud to your child. Run your finger under the words as you read.

In a land far away there lived three sisters. The youngest sister, Cinderella, was always busy working. Her two older sisters were bossy and they didn't work at all.
"Sweep the floor, Cinderella," said the bossy sisters.
Poor Cinderella!

8

Step 2
Look at the pictures and talk about what is happening.

Step 3

Read the simple text on the right-hand page together. When reading, some words come up again and again, such as **the**, **to**, **and**. Your child will quickly get to recognize these high-frequency words by sight.

Cinderella had to stay at home and do all the work.

9

Step 4

When your child is ready, encourage them to read the simple lines on their own.

Step 5

Help your child to complete the puzzles at the back of the book.

In a land far away there lived
three sisters. The youngest sister,
Cinderella, was always busy
working. Her two older sisters
were bossy and they didn't work
at all.

"Sweep the floor, Cinderella,"
said the bossy sisters.

Poor Cinderella!

Cinderella had to stay at home
and do all the work.

One day, a letter arrived. It was from the prince in the big palace and it said: *Please come to the ball.*

"Can I go to the ball?" asked Cinderella.

"No, you must finish your work," said one bossy sister.

"You must help us get ready for the ball!" said the other bossy sister.

Cinderella was sad. She wanted to go and have fun, too.

Please come to the ball.

Cinderella helped her bossy
sisters put on their best dresses.
A coach took them to the
big palace. Cinderella did
all the work at home.
Then she sat alone by
the fire and sobbed.

All of a sudden, a funny
little fairy appeared.

"Who are you?" Cinderella asked.

13

"I am your fairy godmother," said the fairy. "Why are you crying?"

"I can't go to the ball," cried Cinderella. "I haven't got a dress."

The fairy godmother took Cinderella into the garden. She waved her magic wand... and Cinderella had a pretty new dress!

"You can go to the ball now," said the fairy godmother.

15

"But I haven't got a coach," said Cinderella. The fairy godmother waved her wand again... and a magic coach appeared! Now she was ready to go to the ball.

"You must come home before the clock strikes midnight," said the fairy godmother.

"The magic will stop at midnight,"
said the fairy godmother.

When Cinderella arrived at the ball, everyone turned to look at her. "Will you dance with me?" asked the prince. Cinderella danced with the prince all night. The bossy sisters were very cross.

The prince liked Cinderella a lot.

Bong! Suddenly, the clock struck midnight! Cinderella ran away before the magic ended. Her little shoe came off on the steps. "Wait!" called the prince.

The prince ran after her. He saw
the little shoe.

The next day, there was a knock on the door. It was the prince!

"I would like to marry the girl who fits this little shoe," he said. The bossy sisters rushed to put on the shoe. But it was much too little for their big feet.

"Who else lives here?" asked the prince.

"Can I try?" asked Cinderella.

"No, you must finish your work," said the bossy sisters.

"Everyone must try," said the prince. Then the prince gave Cinderella the little shoe.

Cinderella put on the shoe. "It fits!" she said.

Cinderella and the prince were married. The bossy sisters were very cross. Now they had to do all their own work!

The prince gave Cinderella a hug.
They were very happy.

Puzzle time!

Which two words rhyme?

sad   can   fun   run   hug

Which word does not match
the picture?

magic

wand

shoe

Which word matches the picture?

click

clock

cluck

28